ADVENTURE UNDER THE SEA!!

Artist：Keung Chi Kit
（編繪：姜智傑）

Contents

Hi!

Oh~~~ What a sunny day, the temperature is just nice! So comfortable~~

25°C

你好！ 噢~~~今天天朗氣清，氣溫宜人！很舒服啊~~

In such good weather,

I should do some outdoor activities!

天氣這麼好， 應該做點戶外活動！

Ah?

啊？

Oh yeah, why don't we go fishing!

Meow~~

啊，不如去釣魚吧！ 喵~~

Anyone interested !?

大家有興趣嗎!?

3

Adventure under the sea!! (Part 1)

海底王國歷險記（1）

我不喜歡吃魚，
也不會殺生。

我不去了……

外面很曬，會曬傷我的皮膚
和令我的臉長出雀斑。

我不去了~~

我仍有很多書要看，
沒有空啊。

法律

Chaozhou Forest

既然大家都沒有興趣
和我去釣魚……

好……

我自己一個人去吧!!

也能在海中心享受寧靜！
太好了!!

我要去　　　呵　　你不是在屋頂睡覺嗎!?
怎麼突然起來了!?

釣~~~　　　　釣~~~

大~~~　　　　魚~~~~

好吃　　　　　還以為能一個人去，享受
自己的時間⋯⋯嗚⋯⋯

就是這樣，森巴和剛仔　　對！
開始了海底冒險之旅！

7

哈哈，在這種好天氣下釣魚，真寫意啊!!

森巴，　　　　　　　　　　　　你有收穫嗎？

我就知道你會睡着了！
那怎麼會知道有魚上釣!?

有魚上釣

呵~~~

看，魚餌都被吃掉了……

釣魚要專注和有耐性，

一旦發現有魚吃餌，就立刻拉起魚竿，明白嗎？

我示範給你看！

9

啊！有了!! 　　　　　　　伏一

嘩　　　　　　　　嘩!! 好大的魚!!

你看，有耐性就能釣到魚了。　　　　刺身 刺身

世上沒有　　　　伏一　　　想吃就自己　　呀～～
不勞而獲的，　　　　　　　去釣吧！

嘩!! 我又釣到了!!

這條石斑魚應該超過3公斤吧!!

嗚~~~

吼~~~　　你在幹甚麼，森巴!?

呀!! 伏一

啪一

你不會游泳,這樣很危險!!
快回到船上!!

噗~~

嘎~~~~~~ 咘咘咘咘咘咘

What's wrong with you!? Why are you passing gas into the sea!?
FFFF~~~
FFFF~~~
FFFF~~~
!!
Wow ~~~
你幹甚麼!? 為何在海中放屁!? 呠~~~ 呠~~~ 呠~~~

嘩~~~

Sashimi
Sashimi
Sashimi
Sashimi
How can you use such a disgusting method to catch all these seafood?!
!!
刺 身 刺 身

你怎可以用這個噁心的方法來捉這些海鮮?!

Bluhhhhh~~~~~
Your foul gas has made all the seafood stinky!! How could we eat that!?
Ha ~~~
嘔~~~~~

你的屁把海鮮都弄臭了!! 怎麼吃啊!? 哈~~~

啪啪~　　我把你的氣門封了，
　　　　禁止你再污染海洋!!

嗚~~

隆—　　咦？為何突然翻起大浪？

好臭啊~~~~　　　　　　　　　　　　　　蓬—

噗—　　　　　啊~~　　　　　　　　　啪—

誰在海中放毒氣!?

哇~~海怪啊!!

我

啪~   是你!?

哈~~~~~   啪~   噢

咬

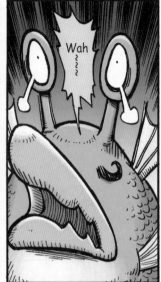

哇~~~

好硬

伏~~

哇~~~ 停啊！我不是給你吃的!!

噢~~~

嘿一

啪一

森巴!!你沒事吧!?

嚼嚼好吃

哇~~~ 你咬下了我魚尾的一塊肉~~!!

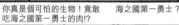

你真是個可怕的生物！竟敢　海之國第一勇士？
吃海之國第一勇士的肉!?

沒錯!!　哇~~~

噗一　　　啊！

潑~~~

17

吐！

咦？森巴在哪!?

掉下水了嗎!?
他不會游泳啊!!

剛

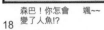

森巴！你怎會
變了人魚!?
颯~~

他變了人魚是因為吃了我的肉!!

18

吼~~~

我要吃回你們的肉作為補償!! 哇~~~

請不要吃我,與我無關啊,海怪大人!!

停手,菲比斯!!

你記得我們為何要上陸地嗎?

我們不能在海面上惹麻煩!

知道了,公主殿下。

啊?

唏~~~

終於到了……

哇~~~ 這裏就是海洋的表面!!

很漂亮啊!!

她……她就是公主殿下!?

很美啊……

哈

Adventure under the sea!! (Part 2)
海底王國歷險記（2）

哇~~~這是我第一次   肥 魚   為甚麼會有個女孩子   完全超乎我想像!!
看到海面的世界……!!   從海怪口裏走出來？

呀!?

来自陆地的人类，
你好吗？　　　噢？你问我吗？

当然！你是我第一个见到的
陆地人！你叫甚么名字？　　　呀!!

我……　　　　　　　　　　　　　　　我的名字是……

森巴　　　呀~~~　　　　　　　　　涮—

啊~~~你很可爱!!　　你好

嘿~~~~~

咳咳~~ 好險，我差點兒淹死……

哈哈，那個野人是我弟弟。有嚇着你嗎？　　　沒……沒有……

在下龍小剛，今年13歲，身高146厘米，　　　　　　　　　　　　為一名品學兼優的學生，興趣是結交新朋友和……

Pew

噴

Ha ~~~

I warn you Samba!

Stop spoiling my "good looking"!

哈~~~ 森巴，我警告你！ 不要在我耍帥的時候掃我的興！

Haha, you two are really interesting ~~~

哈哈，你們兩個真有趣~~~

I've been all alone in the palace,

I'm so bored... I have no siblings to play with...

我一個人住在皇宮裏， 很悶呀……沒有兄弟姊妹陪我玩……

Oh! I haven't introduced myself,

my name is Luna, I'm the 12th generation princess of the Mermaid Kingdom under the sea!

噢！我還未介紹自己， 我叫露娜，是來自海底的人魚之國第12代公主。

Mer-maid

You're from the sea kingdom!?

人魚 你來自海底王國!?

That's right!! And I am from a race of giant frog-fish,

the bodyguard of the princess ~~~~

Wah

對!!而我是來自巨蛙魚族，

哇

是公主的保鏢~~~~

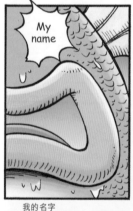

My name

我的名字

is

叫

Phelps

菲比斯

Eh ~~~

唔~~~

Why did you stand so suddenly!? You almost made me fall to my death!!

Sor ... sorry ... princess ...

幹嗎忽然站起來!?
幾乎令我跌死了!!

對……對不起……
公主……

你斗膽做多次，我就辭退你!! 　知……知道…… 　看來，最強勇士都有他的弱點…… 　　嗖— 　總算找到你了!!

我從遠處就聽到你大叫呀，菲比斯！ 　　今次我不會讓你輕易逃脫!! 　　沙—

他們來自惡魚軍團!! 　　啊!!這回糟了!! 　　哇~~~來了些兇惡的魚~~~

嗚!!

不能呼吸……　　　救命~~~

救我，菲比斯~~~

要淹死了……

啪一

快，我們游回海面吧!!　　　露娜!?

伏—哇~~

你還活着就好了，剛仔！

那些奇怪的魚是來捉我的，不過無論如何，我都不會讓你受牽連!!

所以我會保護你!!
我不會讓你受到傷害!!

露娜

嗆~~

露娜公主，乖乖地跟我們回到海裏，不然，別怪我用武力對待!!

可惡呀!!

作為人魚之國的公主

我不會輕易背叛我的王國!!

去捉他們！ 有本事就來捉我!!

森巴~~

森巴，你還好？ 肥魚

我沒事

吥 吥 吥 吥

呵 吥— 不要再在海裏 幸好他咬了我一口，才可以
放毒氣!! 在海裏活動自如……

森巴，我們要保護公主！
跟我來！

是

吼~~~你想救公主，
就必須先打倒我！

呀!!是魔鬼魚!!

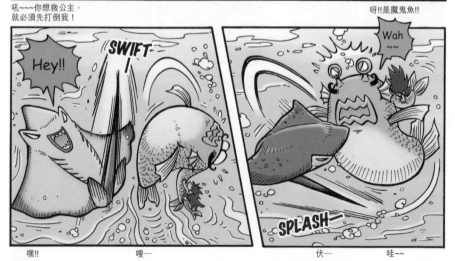

嘿!!

嗖一

伏一

哇~~

嘿

我又玩

你好

呵~~　　　啊~~!!

伏一　　　好痛呀~~~!!

哼

呵

伏一　　　　　　走開，小子!!

哇~~~

讓你嘗嘗我的毒刺吧!!　　　　嗖一

刺~~~

Hehehe, you've been stabbed by my stinger, you'll be paralysed and doomed in less than 10 seconds...

嘿嘿嘿，你中了我的毒刺，
不出10秒就會全身麻痺而死⋯⋯

What !?

甚麼!?

A poisonous pufferfish !?

毒河豚!?

Hehehe, that's right!

This purple pufferfish is 10 times more poisonous than your stinger!!

嘿嘿嘿，對!

這是比你的毒刺毒10倍的
紫河豚!!

Wah ~~~ help me get rid of it!!

哇~~~幫我弄走牠呀!!

哇~~~救我!!牠的毒素開始傳過來了!!

我快要死了~~~

啪—

咦!?

森巴，你在做甚麼!?

拜

為甚麼要救他？
他會殺害我們的!!

吼~~~

37

嗚~~~小朋友多謝你救了我~~~

再見！ 拜

不然我已經中毒身亡~~~

我為剛剛對你做的事道歉，
但我也是受人指使才這樣……

我以後不會再騷擾你們~~~

真是個不可思議的孩子。他竟然可以馴服
一隻如此危險的魔鬼魚……難道他是……

是我們要尋找的……

救世者!?

但……他看來
不太像……

Adventure under the sea!! (Part 3)
海底王國歷險記（3）

嘎~~~嘎~~~

公主，我勸你投降吧!! 別再幹蠢事了!!

嗖—

嘎……可惡啊!! 他們追上我們了……

Ah!! There's land up ahead!!

啊!!前面有陸地!!

Though I'm not sure what will happen...

雖然不知道會有甚麼事發生……

But for the Mermaid Kingdom and Kang's sake, I have to give it a try!

但為了人魚之國和剛仔,唯有試一試!

SWISH

Ah!

嗖—

呀!

Hey—

PA

啪—　嘿—

?

噢—

噗—

哇～～　很痛呀～～～

啊!!　　　　　　　　　　　　　　　　　是沙!!

I've never felt dry sand before!!

So this is what land feels like!? Kang!!

Eh? Where's Kang?

Arrrr... I'm here...

Wah!!

我之前都沒見過沙!!

這就是陸地上的感覺!? 剛仔!!

咦？剛仔呢？

嗚……我在這裏……

哇!!

Huff!! What's going on here?

Why am I here? Shouldn't I be under the sea!?

Kang!! Are you ok?

!!

嘎!! 發生了甚麼事？

為何會在這裏？我不是在海底吧!?

剛仔!! 你沒事吧？

I'm fine, don't worry.

I just scratched my forehead a bit.

CLANK

Again!?

我沒事，放心吧。

只是頭有點擦傷而已。

噹——

又來!?

可惡，居然走到 別以為這樣就能 呀！ 公主!!我們走進
陸地上!! 逃離我們!! 沙— 森林吧!!

哼，我們就包圍 我不認為她能在 只要令公主無法在 人魚之國就會落入
著這個島!! 陸地上待很久!! 限期內回到皇宮， 我們惡魚軍團手中!!

嘿嘿嘿嘿嘿嘿~~~~~

44

好！大家分頭包圍小島！

別讓公主有機會回到海底！

可惡！公主被他們趕到荒島上！

她不能在沒有水的環境下待超過10分鐘！

森巴！我們要儘快趕走惡魚，保護公主！

好

決鬥

喂！等等!!

他們人多勢眾，而且我的力量又被森巴削弱了……

恐怕我這個海底最強勇士也贏不了他們。

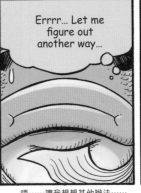

唔……讓我想想其他辦法……

喂

45

我去

引開他們

你去救公主　　　　　啊！

我明白了！森巴偽裝成惡魚
軍團的人，做臥底引開他們！

這小子年紀雖小，但很聰明!!
他果然是我們要找的救星!!

吱 吱 吱

哈~~~~~很癢呀!!
啊！不要搔我!!

甚麼？誰搔你？

呵~~~

喂！你是誰？
你在海底幹甚麼!?

朋友

咦？你是我軍團的人？
好像沒見過你⋯⋯

可惡！他們發現了森巴！
這次麻煩了⋯⋯

那邊有很多魚吃

跟我來吧

真的？

Hold on!

等等！

Though you look like one of us, something about you is "fishy"!

雖然你長得像我們，但不足以令我們相信你！

You need to pass a test to prove you're from our army!

你要通過測試，證明你是我們軍團的人！

SWISH~~

!!

伏~~

What's your name?

!!

你叫甚麼名字？

......

......

Can't tell them the real name, but can't think of another name...

不能說真名，但又想不到另一個名字……

Never mind, you low ranking fish from the bad fish army don't have any names anyway... you just passed the test!!

Phew...

不要緊，我們惡魚軍團的最低層小卒是沒有名字的……測試通過!!

嘎……

好，事不宜遲，魚在哪裏？
快帶我們去吧！　　　好

跟我來　　　　　　　　　　　啪—

呀~~

呀！我認得你!!　　　你是菲比斯身邊的小子!!　　哈~~~~~　　露餡

Run

Don't let him escape!!

Wah ~~~

逃　　　別讓他逃掉!!　　　哇~~~

Don't try to escape ~~~

別走~~~

Brothers, go get him!!

Well done Samba!! You've managed to distract all of them!

各位兄弟，一起追!!　　　做得好，森巴!!你引開了他們！

Just like the prophecy said,

Samba is the brave warrior who will help us regain the Mermaid Kingdom!

就像預言書所説，　　　森巴是幫我們奪回人魚之國的勇士！

Alright! I have to go save the princess now!!

好！那我去救公主了!!

Huff ~~~~ It's really hot on land...

I think they're unable to catch us this deep inside the woods!

嘎~~~~地面真的很熱啊……

在這森林深處，他們應該無法抓到我們了！

Those bad fishes aren't trying to catch me...

They just want to keep me here so that they will have time to seize the throne...

Huh?

Let me explain. You see...

......

那些惡魚的目的並不是要抓我……

他們只想把我困在這裏，那就有時間去奪取皇位……

咦？

我給你解釋吧……

Mermaid Kingdom is thousands of miles deep beneath the sea,

it's an isolated place unknown to humans.

人魚之國是位於幾千哩的深海，

一直與世隔絕，從未被人發現。

We, the Mermaids, have been living there peacefully for thousands of years,

in harmony with all other species.

我們人魚族幾千年來都過着安穩的生活，

與其他海洋族羣和平共處。

51

The Mermaid army has always kept the peace, preventing the bad fish from invading.

全靠人魚之國的軍隊維持治安，防止任何有惡意的魚類入侵。

This is the task of a great Mermaid, the supreme commander of the army, General Cayman. His army has been guarding the Mermaids from generation to generation... For hundreds of years, they were always loyal, until...

其中最重要的就是軍隊的最高統帥，凱曼將軍。

幾百年來，他的軍隊都守護着人魚族，忠心耿耿，直至……

Well, my father will soon be 500 years old, and according to tradition, he needs to pass the throne to the next heir, and the only one fit to inherit the throne, is his only daughter...

由於父皇快到五百歲，根據傳統，他要將皇位傳給下一位繼承人，

而繼承者只有一個，就是他唯一的女兒……

So that's you, Princess Luna!?

Yes, but...

就是露娜公主你吧!?

對，可是……

not everyone is glad to see me take the throne...

不是每個人都樂於看到我繼承皇位……

Two days ago, General Cayman led all his men on a siege on the palace,

he said he wanted to abolish the throne succession, he felt that whoever had all the power should be king instead.

兩日前，凱曼將軍率領所有部下包圍皇宮，

他說要廢除皇位繼任，應該由擁有最大權力的人成為國皇。

Facing General Cayman's army of 3000 men, the 10 guards of the palace couldn't even a fight,

and the palace soon fell.

面對凱曼將軍的三千人軍隊，皇宮中僅有的十名侍衛根本無法招架，　皇宮一下子失守。

And I was imprisoned so that I couldn't go out on father's birthday...

under the law, the absence of an official successor meant that the throne would be "legally" passed to General Cayman.

而我則被囚禁，令我在父皇大壽那日不可以出去…

在沒有正式繼承人的情況下，皇位就會「合法地」傳給凱曼將軍。

Fortunately, Phelps launched a rescue at the prison last night,

and he managed to save me from the cage.

幸好，菲比斯昨晚偷襲監牢，　救了我離開。

In order to save Mermaid Kingdom, we decided to swim to the surface of the sea,

and find the legendary brave warrior who will save us all...

為了拯救人魚之國，我們決定游到海面，

尋找傳說中拯救國家的勇者……

That's where I met you Kang...

Well... Where is this legendary warrior of yours?

之後就遇到剛仔你們了……

那……你要找的勇者在哪裏？

Prin-cess!!

公主!!

Ar gh hh ~~~

Princess, what happened? Are you OK?

呀~~~

公主，怎麼了？你沒事吧？

W... water ~~~

Ah !!

水……水呀~~~

呀!!

I see, Luna needs the sea, without water, she can't breathe or move, she cannot last long without it...

我明白了，露娜需要水，沒有水她就無法呼吸和行動，支持不了多久……

I have to find some water for Luna,

but where on earth can I find water here!?

我要找點水給露娜，

但在陸地上哪裏有水!?

啊!!是椰子樹!!

呀……

公主!別放棄!
我很快就會拿水給你!!

唏~~~!!

呀~~~~

啪—

呀,很痛啊~~~~!!!

森巴在就好了……

水……水呀……

露娜公主……

我一定會救你的!!

嘿!!再來!!

碰—

嗚~~

Heee~~~
Haaa~~~

啼~~~呀~~~

Huffff
~~
Almost
there...

嘎~~就到了……

This is my
first time
climbing to
the top of
a tree...

這是我第一次爬到樹頂呀……

CLACK

CLACK

啪—   啪—

Phew~~ finally I removed all the coconuts,

the princess can drink the coconut water!

嘎~~終於摘下所有椰子，   公主可以飲椰子水了！

Oh no!! I don't dare to go down ...

Whoa! So high...

Wah~~~ help!! Somebody help me get down!!

Kang!!

嚇！好高……   弊!!我不敢下去……   哇~~~救命呀!!找人來救我下去呀!!   剛仔!!

Huff ~~~

I finally found you!!

Phelps !!

嘎~~~   我總算找到你了!!   菲比斯!!

Adventure under the sea!! (Part 4)
海底王國歷險記（4）

Pew
!!

吐!!

PA

Argh
~

啪— 呀~~

Humph! The fish here are getting more and more tasteless!!

The Mermaid Kingdom's sea must have gotten polluted!

哼！這裏的魚愈來愈乏味!!

肯定是人魚之國的
海水受到污染了！

But never mind, if the princess doesn't show up in 40 minutes...

Your throne will be taken over by me!!

但不要緊，只要公主沒在40分鐘之內出現……

你的皇位就會由我來繼承!!

Then I will govern this kingdom and solve the water pollution problem for you!

我將管治這個王國，
並替你解決水污染的問題！

Humph! My daughter will definitely come back here to save me. And then, she will finish you traitor!!

哼！我女兒一定會回來救我。
那時候，她會收拾你這個叛徒!!

Hehehe, I'll just wait and see when the princess will make her appearance here!

嘿嘿嘿，那我就等着，
看公主甚麼時候在這裏現身！

Just watch her get easily defeated by this hand of mine!!

待我用這隻手把她輕易擊敗。

SLASH

砰—

SLASH

啪—

PHEW
～～～

Drink it slowly, princess ～～

I still have a lot for you!

GULP GULP ～～

嗄～～　吞吞～～　　公主，慢慢喝吧～～

我還有很多給你的！

CRACK

哐—

Ha～～～ the coconut water here is so delicious ～～

Thank you for climbing up to the tree and picking the coconut for me, Kang!

哈～～～這椰子水很美味呀～～

多謝你爬上樹摘這些椰子給我，剛仔！

Ha ha, you're welcome !!

No matter how risky it may be, I will do my best for you, princess!

哈哈，不用客氣!!

無論有多危險，我都會盡全力幫公主你的！

I'm really glad to have met you here!

Oh I'm melting...

能在這裏遇到你真是太好了！

噢，我溶化了……

Princess! There's no time for us to chit-chat!!

SLAP

WAHH ～～～

公主！我們沒時間閒聊!!

啪—　　哇～～～

63

Even you're in a hurry, you don't have to punch me so hard!!

Phelps!!

就算你趕時間，也不用這麼用力打我吧!!

Huh!?

菲比斯!!

啊!?

Pant

嘎……

Ahhh~~ Phelps, why did your body shrink so much? You're smaller now!!

Pant... I'm dehydrating...

Hang on! Let me grab more coconuts for you!

啊~~菲比斯，怎麼你的身體收縮了？你變細了!!

嘎……我在脱水呀……

支持住！我去摘些椰子給你！

Forget it, there's no time already...

不用了，已經沒時間……

I've already found the warrior who is able to save Mermaid Kingdom. The most important thing to do now, is to get back to the sea as soon as possible...

Huh!?

我已經找到可以拯救人魚之國的勇者。現在最重要的是，儘快回到海裏……

吓!?

THUD

Ahh Phelps!!

Hang on!! I'll take you back to the sea real soon...

啪— 呀！菲比斯!!

撑着呀!!我很快就把你带回海裏……

WAH!!

SWIFT

That's the princess screaming!! What happened!?

Wah ~~~

Phelps-HP -164

哇!! 伏— 是公主的喊聲!!發生甚麼事!? 哇~~~ 菲比斯生命值-164

Wahhh~~ there's an ugly land creature!! Don't come closer to me~~!!

Errr ~~~

哇~~ 好醜的陸地生物呀!!不要靠近我~~!! 嗚~~~

Unforgivable ... don't be rude to my princess!

DONG

豈有此理……不得對公主無禮！ 咥—

Princess, don't worry, this land creature will not harm you!

Wahhh~~ th... there are so many ......

公主，放心，這種陸地生物不會傷害你的！

呀~~很……很多……

Huh?

How many!?

吓？

有很多嗎!?

EEK EEK~~

EEK~~~~

Wah~~~

嗚嗚~~~

嗚~~~~

哇~~

EEK!!

嗚!!

They look pretty upset that we drank their coconut water...

Th... then what should we do now!?

他們看來頗不滿我們喝了這些椰子水……

那……我們現在怎麼辦!?

Hoooo~~~~

嗚~~~~

嗚~~~　　　嗚~~~　　　走呀~~~!!!

嘎……我……我要水~~~

抓一　　　　　　　　　呀~~~

跑快些!!　　　　　　哇~~~

見到海了!!　　　　公主，捉緊我的手!!

跳呀!!　　　　　　　　　嗖—　　　　　嗚~~　　　　　抓~~

噗~~

嘎~~　　　　　　　　　　　　　　　　　嘎~~

Yeah! We got rid of them!!

Ha~~ fortunately, these monkeys don't know how to swim!

太好了！我們擺脫他們了!!

哈~~幸好那些猴子不會游泳！

Yeah I'm saved!!

WAH

我復活了!!

哇~~

The sea world is the only place where I belong.

海洋世界是唯一適合我的地方。

Good to know that you're better Phelps!!

But please don't jump out like that again or I'll kick you! You just gave me a fright!!

你復元了真好，菲比斯!!

但請你別再這樣子跳出來，否則就革你職！把我嚇死了!!

Princess, it's time for us to go back to the Mermaid Kingdom...

公主，我們是時候回去人魚之國……

So you found the warrior who will save Mermaid Kingdom?

即是你已經找到可以拯救人魚之國的勇者？

That's right! It's all thanks to him for distracting those villainous fishes so that I could go ashore to find you.

I think he's still near the sea, let's go help him deal with those bad fish!

沒錯！全靠他去引開那羣惡魚，我才可以上岸找回你們。

我想他仍在附近的海裏，一起去幫他對付惡魚吧！

Phew

嘎～～～

Could Samba be the warrior that Phelps was talking about?

Ah! Samba!

Bye

bye

呀！森巴！

拜拜

難道森巴就是菲比斯口中的勇者？

Aren't you being chased by those fish? Why do you look so relaxed now?

He cannot remember what just happened at all...

你不是被惡魚追嗎？怎麼現在很輕鬆似的？

他記不起剛才做過甚麼……

Ah!

呀！

哈~~~

Such battling spirit is indeed out of the ordinary!

Isn't that the shark that we met quite a long time ago?

You dealt with 12 villainous fish all by yourself!? That's amazing ~~~

Ha ~~~

那是我們在很久以前
遇過的那條鯊魚嗎？

你一個人對付12條
惡魚!?好厲害呀~~~

這股戰鬥精神
確實非同凡響！

噢！即是説森巴就是
我們要找的勇者？

對呀，公主！

今次，人魚之國
有希望了！

這完全跟我猜
的一樣……

好吧！時間無多！

我們向人魚之國出發吧！

出發~~~!!

等等！

我在水裏無法呼吸~~~~
怎樣能到到目的地!?

嗚~~~

呀!?

72

Adventure under the sea!! (Part 5)
海底王國歷險記（5）

I almost forgot that you're unable to breathe in the sea!

我差點兒忘了你不能在海裏呼吸！

Don't worry, let me help you.

不用擔心，我來幫你。

INHALE~~

吸氣~~

SWIFT~~~

伏~~~

Blow~~~~~

呼~~~~

74

BLOW

呼~~~~

哈哈~~~這是人魚族
的特殊能力。

我可以用體內的氧氣，製造
一個大氣泡讓你能呼吸！

Ah!

啊！

Oxygen? How am I able to breathe again now!?

Haha~~~ that's the special mermaid power,

I can use the oxygen inside my body and create a big bubble for you to breathe!

是氧氣？怎麼我
又能呼吸了!?

But we don't usually use this technique on anyone,

the person must be very close to us and trust-worthy!

但我們不會隨便對
任何人用這個技能，

對象一定是非常親密
和值得信任的人！

So this is the oxygen that Luna exhale...

No wonder it smells sweet and lovely ~~~

所以這是露娜
呼出的氧氣……

難怪聞起來甜蜜
又令人愉快~~

Does this mean that some special relation-ship between me and Luna will...

這是説，我和露娜之間
將發展成特別關係……

75

POP

噇——

Samba! Why did you puncture my bubble?!

Bubble

Bubble

森巴！你為甚麼刺穿我的氣泡?!　　泡 泡

Grrrrrr~~~ I cannot breathe again...

Help......

嗚~~~我又不能呼吸了……　　救命呀……

BLOW~

Luna!?

呼~~~~　　露娜!?

Blow~~~~

My lung capacity is big, so this bubble is enough to sustain you for a whole day!

But, I've been eating too much sea urchin recently, so the smell may be a bit bad...

呼~~~~　　我的肺容量大，所以這個氣泡足以維持一整天!　　但是，我最近吃了太多海膽，口氣可能有點差……

76

Arrrrr

呀~~~~

Alright! Let's continue the journey!

好！我們繼續上路吧！

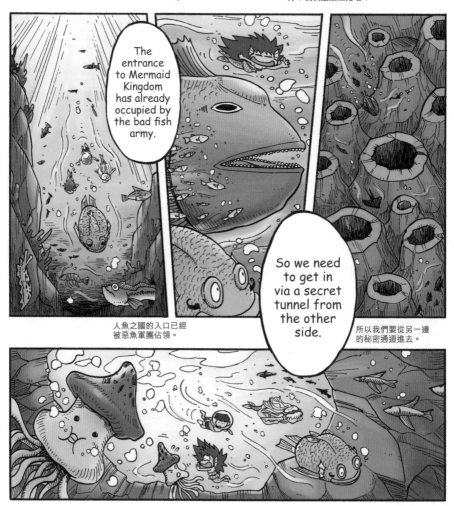

The entrance to Mermaid Kingdom has already occupied by the bad fish army.

人魚之國的入口已經被惡魚軍團佔領。

So we need to get in via a secret tunnel from the other side.

所以我們要從另一邊的秘密通道進去。

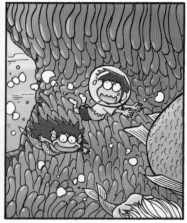
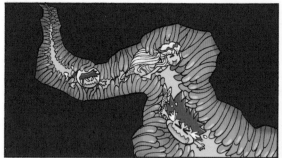

Wow, the scenery here is awesome~~~

Welcome to the Mermaid Kingdom!

This is the coral district at the border of Mermaid Kingdom. Here, the security system is not that strict.

And that is the palace!

哇，真令人讚歎的景致~~~　歡迎來到人魚之國！

這裏是人魚之國邊境的珊瑚區。
此處的守衛戒備沒那麼森嚴。

那就是皇宮！

In order to sneak into the palace, we'd better be very careful.

Come into my mouth, I'll bring you to the palace!

Huh!?

Wow

Erm... this makes me feel uncomfortable...

Go

唔……這讓我感覺很不舒服……　去

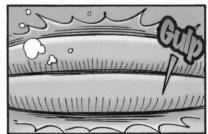

Gulp

為了順利潛入皇宮，
必須十分小心。　到我的口裏，
我載你們去皇宮！　哇　吓!?　合一

看來這後門沒重兵防守……

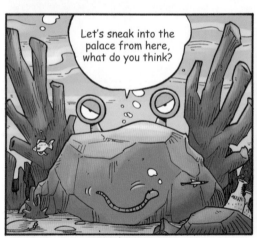

我們就從這邊潛入皇宮，
大家有意見嗎？

你先把我們放出去，
在裏面甚麼都看不到！

哈……

Haha~~ sorry about that.... I'm really nervous.

Though here only was two security guards, we cannot break in abruptly,

otherwise, reinforcements will come...

哈哈~~抱歉……
我太緊張了。

雖然這裏只有兩個守衛，
但我們不能硬闖，

否則，會引來
援兵……

You're right, princess!

We should stay calm and wait for the right time to sneak in!

Kang!

Break

in

你說得對， 剛仔！
公主！

我們應該保持安靜和
等待適當時機潛入去！

潛入

I said to stay calm! Why did you have to make such a ruckus?!

Do you want them to discover our plan!?

Oh, I got an idea! We can disguise ourselves!

That's a brilliant idea!

我說要保持安靜！
你怎麼在喧鬧?!

你是想被他們
發現我們嗎!?

噢，我有個主意！
我們可以喬裝自己！

好聰明的主意！

81

First, Kang and Samba dress up as their security guards.

And I will hide inside Phelps's mouth.

首先，剛仔和森巴扮成他們的守衛。

而我就躲在菲比斯的口裏。

Then Phelps will be tied up, and he can pretend to pass out.

然後將菲比斯綁起，並假裝暈倒。

Later, Kang and Samba, you will "escort" Phelps to the General, so you can gain access to the palace.

之後，剛仔和森巴，你們去把菲比斯「押送」給將軍，從而獲准進入皇宮。

When they see that Phelps is captured, they won't suspect anything.

當他們看到菲比斯被捉住，便不虞有詐。

So we can successfully enter the palace and save my father!

我們就順利進入皇宮，救出父皇！

公主真聰明！ 我們就按你的計劃行事吧！

不要擋路~ 碰——

森巴，你呢!?

哼！煩人的魚！

好，我裝備好了！ 看來沒甚麼變化……

你的造型沒半點兒像任何一個惡魚守衛!!

Here, this looks more suitable!

· · · · ·

看，這樣更合適！

Alright! We're well prepared. Just not sure if Phelps is ready too...

?

好！我們準備好了。不知道
菲比斯準備好了沒⋯⋯

Is he pretending to be passed out, or is he actually asleep...?

Ho~~~

喝~~~

他是假裝暈去，
抑或真的睡了⋯⋯？

Maybe he has been too worn out these two days, so he fell asleep right away when he lay down...

看來他在這兩天累透了，
所以一躺下來就睡了⋯⋯

Luckily we're in the sea, so he's not too heavy to carry...

HA~~~

Zzz

幸好我們在海裏，搬起來
也不會太重⋯⋯

哈~~~

Alright! Let's move!

好！行動開始！

This section of the palace is off limits! No one is allowed to enter!

Who are you!?

這裏是皇宮禁地！
任何人等不得內進！

你們是
甚麼人!?

I am Sam-

We are your companions! We're from the bad fish army too!

我 是 森-

我們是你們的同伴！
我們也來自惡魚軍團！

We just caught the princess personal bodyguard, Phelps.

And I'm ordered to give him to General Cayman in the palace.

我們剛捉到公主的
私人保鏢，菲比斯。

現正奉命把他帶入
皇宮交給凱曼將軍。

Huh?

Is it true?

啊？

真有其事？

Was he really caught by you?

他真的是你們捉的？

Ho

Yeah~ we saw him sleeping at the coral district, so we launched a sneak attack and caught him!

喝

是呀~ 我們看到他在珊瑚區睡着了，於是就發動偷襲並捕捉他！

Stab ≀≀≀

刺~~

......

Looks like he really fainted...

Luckily Phelps is sleeping really deeply...

他看來真的暈了……

幸好菲比斯睡得很沉……

好啦！快把他帶去給凱曼將軍。

感謝！

但是你們不可以經這門口進去!!

吓!?

這後門太小，像他這種大魚沒法子穿過！

糟了！我們從沒想過這點！

我們帶你到皇宮的正門吧！

吓？

也來幫你搬這大魚。

哇~~ 我們自己搬就可以了!!

Phew~ It looks like we are back to the drawing board again...

嗄~看樣子我們還是用了
最原始的方法去解決……

Ah~~~ sorry about falling asleep just now...what did I miss?

......

啊~~~抱歉剛剛睡着了……
我有錯過甚麼嗎？

Adventure under the sea!! (Part 6)
海底王國歷險記（6）

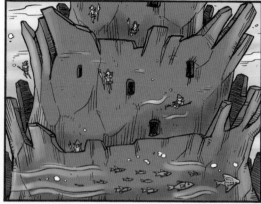

人魚之國的女士們和先生們，大家好！

歡迎來到新一任人魚之國國皇
的登基典禮!!

今日我很榮幸可以主持
這個重要儀式……

I am the new staff officer of the bad fish army,

my name is Lulu and I'm 15 years old...

我是惡魚軍團的新任參謀官，　　我叫魯魯，今年15歲……

Spare us your speech !!

Wah ~~

廢話少講!!　　哇～～

As everyone knows, the king is going to pass his throne to the next heir.

大家都知道，國皇快要將皇位傳給下一位繼承人。

But the princess has been missing in action up till now,

therefore, only I, General Cayman, is capable enough to bear this great mission...

但公主在行動期間失蹤，一直至今，　　所以，惟有我，凱曼將軍，有足夠能力去承擔這個重任……

As long as the three elders bear witness,

I will become the twelfth-generation king!!

在三大長老的見證下，　　我將成為第十二代國皇!!

91

How dare you!! You do not deserve to become the king!!

你敢!!你不配成為國皇!!

You robbed the throne through military force, and even if you become the king, you will never gain our trust!!

用武力奪取皇位的人，就算成為國皇，也永遠得不到人們的信任!!

Security! Drive him out of here!!

Yes!

Wah

守衛！拉他出去!!　　是！　哇~~~

Anyone else who objects will end up like him!

誰有異議下場就和他一樣！

....

Alright, since there's no other objection, let's continue with the ceremony...

好，既然無人有意見，典禮繼續……

所有東西準備好？　　準備好！

好！登基儀式正式開始!!

伏一

完成　　森巴，你就這樣解決他們!?

93

啊~~~~~

你做得到的,菲比斯!

呀~~~我動不了……

怎樣試也進不去啊~~~~!!

嘎~~~

真失敗!怎麼我之前
沒想到?

我身形太大,
根本穿不過這扇門!

嘎~~~

菲比斯,不如你打破
這扇門進去吧!?

No I can't! That would draw attention from the bad fish!

不，不可以！這只會引起惡魚的注意！

You three go into the palace first!

I will stay here and try to stall for time as best as I can. Then I'll find the chance to get in from the main door!

你們三個先入皇宮！

我留守這裏，儘量拖延時間，再找機會從大門進去！

Phelps! That's too dangerous!! There are thousands of soldiers out there patrolling!

菲比斯！這太危險了!! 他們有成千士兵在外面巡邏！

We have no time! The three of you, just go in!

時間無多！你們三個，進去吧！

I know how to deal with them!

Please be careful you guys!

我能應付他們！

你們自己也要小心！

BANG

砰—

Phelps...

Princess, we need to leave as fast as we can!

Don't worry about Phelps, he will be fine!

菲比斯……　　公主，我們要儘快離開！　　別擔心菲比斯，他不會有事的！

……

Ok! Just follow Phelps's plan, we cannot let him down!!

Luna will accomplish the mission!!

好！按菲比斯的計劃去做，我們不可以辜負他！！　　我露娜會完成這個使命！！

Father, I'm here to save you!

Princess! Wait for us!!

父皇，我來救你啊！　　公主！帶上我們啊!!

Ah!

啊！

That's the minister of the environment! Why is he being carried away?

那位是環境大臣！怎麼他會被帶走？

Could the ascension ceremony have started already!?

難道登基儀式已經開始了!?

Kang, Samba! We need to get to the great church at the palace's centre soon!

剛仔，森巴！我們要趕快去皇宮中心的大聖堂！

Where's the great church?

Follow me!

大聖堂在哪兒？　　跟我來！

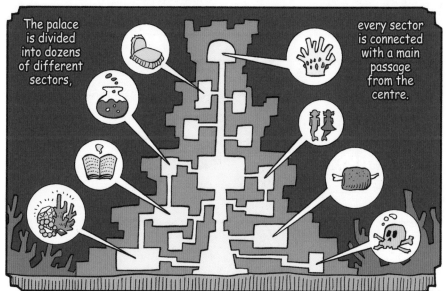

The palace is divided into dozens of different sectors,

every sector is connected with a main passage from the centre.

皇宮分為十多個不同的區域，　　　　　　每個區域都有主要通道與中央連接。

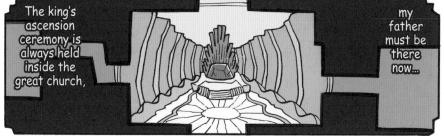

The king's ascension ceremony is always held inside the great church,

my father must be there now...

國皇的登基儀式都是在大聖堂裏進行，

我父皇現在一定在裏面……

97

As long as the three elders of the Mermaid Kingdom gather in front of the ancient imperial stone with the new king and old king,

'and read out the chapter of founding written by the very first king, then the transfer of the throne will officially be completed.

只要人魚之國的三大長老與新舊國皇一齊聚集在古皇石前，

再讀出第一任國皇所寫的立國憲章，就會正式完成皇位交接。

Then, General Cayman will rule all of Mermaid Kingdom.

到時，凱曼將軍將會完全統治人魚之國。

SWIFT

嗖—
擦—

CLACK

Ahh!

Princess!

公主！

呀！

Tsk! We almost hit them!

It's the soldiers from the bad fish army!

噴！差點能擊中他們！

是惡魚軍團的戰士！

公主，你竟敢回來
找你的父親？

你想救他的話，就要先
打敗我們！

可惡……這裏的守衛比
別處更森嚴……

看來我們要硬闖！ 森巴勇者！
要靠你了！

嗨 小朋友？你迷路了嗎？

第1回合 決鬥！

碰—

嗚~~~!!

SWISH—

伏—

Hey

BANG

唏

砰—

SAMBA WINS!!

Samba this isn't the time to show off! Quickly get to the next sector!

森巴勝利!!

森巴,現在不是炫耀時候!
快去下一區!

ROUND 2

STUN GUN SEAHORSE HP 1380

第2回合　　電擊海馬 HP 1380

滋～～

遊戲結束

嘿嘿嘿～～～

滋～～　　　　　　滋～～

過關！

STAGE 3

!!

HAND ROLL TARO

第3回合　　　手卷太郎

トー

PEW

咻

嚐一

過關！

第8回合

第13回合

第21回合　　　　拳擊 腳踢 選項

SWIFT

伏—

Puff~~~~~

嘎~~~~~

Samba, Kang! We're finally here!!

This is the great church!!

森巴，剛仔！
我們終於到了!!

這裏就是大聖堂!!

Hehehe princess, without our permission, no one can enter the place!

嘿嘿嘿，公主殿下，沒經我們
批准，沒有人可以進去！

We are the three coloured warriors of the bad fish!

我們是惡魚三色戰士！

All of you here, please bear witness to this scene. I will be loyal to Mermaid Kingdom and serve all the fishes,

under my authority, I will maintain a peaceful kingdom under the sea forever...

在座各位，請為此儀式作見證。
吾將效忠人魚之國，為所有子民效力，

在吾之權力下，誓必維持一個和平
的海底國度，直到永遠⋯⋯

I, General Cayman do solemnly swear.

我，凱曼將軍謹此宣誓。

General! You can wear the crown and become the new king!

將軍！你可以戴上皇冠，成為新一任國皇了！

Hehe, the whole Mermaid Kingdom will soon be mine...

嘿嘿，人魚之國
即將屬於我了！

Stop right there !!

住手!!

別忘了這裏還有公主，凱曼將軍!!

我不會讓你奸計得逞的!!

露娜公主!?

Adventure under the sea!! (Part 7)
海底王國歷險記（7）

You need to stop it, General Cayman!

I'm taking back the Mermaid Kingdom now!!

收手吧，凱曼將軍！

我是來拿回人魚之國的!!

Father! I'm here to save you!!

父皇！我回來救你了!!

Luna !!

露娜!!

哼!! / 公主，沒想到你會在這裏出現！

凱曼將軍，把皇冠還給我!!

好，還給你吧！反正這對我來説已沒有意義！

嗖— / 就由我這位新任國皇親自解決你吧!!

放馬過來吧!!我已經找到拯救人魚之國的勇者了！

甚麼!?

他就是森巴!!

咦?他在哪?

嗨 長頸魚

哇!! 你對我的皇冠做甚麼~~~

原來你就是勇者?

怎樣看你也只是一條笨魚!

咬

哇~~~

好硬

Go away!

FU—

伏—

走開！

Samba!!

PU—

噗—

森巴!!

Outrageous!!

How dare you stain my most valuable weapon under the sea!

豈有此理!!

竟敢弄髒我這海底最強的武器！

Let me show you its true power!!

BANG

Wah

就讓你見識它的力量吧!!

轟—　　哇～～～

噢— 呀！

嘿~~

粉碎—

呀~~~~

嘿嘿嘿~~~

這是巨型螃蟹的鉗，

整個海底沒有東西比它更硬!!

夾— 呀~~~

嘿嘿嘿~~~

呼—— 森巴！

它的力量甚至
能擊敗鯨魚!!

即使你再強壯，
也不是它的對手!!

認輸吧!!

113

呀~~ 森巴!!

到你們了!!

嘿!! 蓬—— 呀~~

伏—— 凱曼將軍變得瘋狂起來！我們要用其他方法去對付他！

只有一個方法…… 啊，父皇!? 你的意思是……

Tie them all up!

把他們全部捆起來！

Under my rule, no one will go against me!

You are going to spend the rest of your lives in prison!

在我的統治下，沒有人能反抗我！

你們就在監獄裏度過餘生吧！

Alright, today's ceremony ends here, I'm going back to the palace to take a rest.

好，今天的儀式到此為止，我先回寢宮休息一會。

?

Wah~~ Why did the water suddenly turn so black?

I can't see anything!

哇~~為甚麼海水會突然變黑？

我甚麼都看不到！

?

Ahhh

?

Eh? What happened? Why is there so much ink?

呀~~~

咦？發生甚麼事？這麼多墨汁的？

Kang! Quickly leave this place with Samba!

It's the princess's voice!

剛仔！快和森巴離開這裏！

是公主的聲音！

115

跟我父皇走吧！ 她在那裏！ 我會引開他們！ 露娜！

哇~~~ 別過來啊！

露娜，我不會留下你自己走的！

不，你們走吧！ 記得要回來救我啊！

露娜……

國皇，抓到公主了！ 呀!! 是她弄得海中都是墨汁！ 快抓其他人！

剛仔，跟我來！一旦墨汁散開，他們就會發現我們了！ 國皇！

This way!

Luna, you must wait for me!

這邊走！

露娜，你要等我啊！

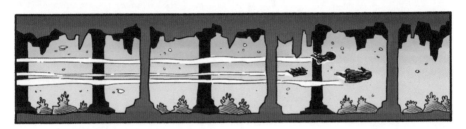

King, where are you taking us to?

To find the only weapon that can defeat General Cayman.

The sword in the stone!!

Sword!?

Huh?

國皇，你要帶我們去哪裏？

去找唯一能對付凱曼將軍的武器。

石中神劍!!

神劍!?　啊

That's a mysterious sword which has been kept in the palace. It is said to have been left by a warrior from the land.

The sword was stuck in a magical stone, and no mermaid could ever pull it out.

那是一直放在皇宮某地方的神秘之劍。
傳說是地上一位勇者遺下的。

這把劍插在一塊大石上，
一直沒有人魚能將它拔出來。

Legend has it that the sword's power is able to defeat anything under the sea,

but only a special warrior can pull it out...

傳說這把劍的威力足以
打敗海底世界的一切，

可是只有一位勇者
能把它拔出來⋯⋯

Ho

So that warrior is Samba?

That's right, with the help of the sword in the stone, Samba will definitely be able to defeat General Cayman!

呵　那位勇者就是
森巴？

沒錯，如果有石中神劍幫忙，
森巴一定能打敗凱曼將軍！

Only the Royal Family knew of the secret passage.

PA—

這是只有皇族
才知道的秘道。

啪—

CLACK

砰—

Here we are, that is the sword in the stone!

我們到了，那就是石中神劍！

So this is it!?

That's right!

就是它!?　　　　　　　　　　　沒錯！

Samba, remove it now!

OK

好　森巴，快把它拔出來！

咿~~~~~~

嘆—

好難啊

It's so difficult

Huh? How could it be?

Maybe Samba is too tired. Why not take some rest first and try again later.

咦？怎會這樣的？

可能森巴太累了，不如
休息一下再試試吧。

10分鐘後……　　　　　　　　呀~~~~~　　　　咬~~~

森巴，加油啊！

咔咔—　　　　　　　　　　　　　　　　呀~~~~~

森巴！你怎能在這個 嘎~~~ 很舒服 呼~~~
神聖的地方大便!!

噗~~

噗~~~

Huh? His fish tail is gone!

Could it be that the effect of Phelps flesh is fading!?

咦?他的魚尾消失了!

難道是菲比斯肉的效果在消退?

Wah~~ Samba can't breathe! Please save him!

哇~~ 森巴無法呼吸!
快救他啊!

PHEW~~~~

呼~~~~

It's so close ...

Ha

Samba couldn't pull out the sword, so perhaps he's not the one that we're looking for...

哈~~~~

幸好⋯⋯ 森巴無法拔出神劍,可能他不是我們要找的勇者⋯⋯

Hehe~~ Looks like you found the wrong one!

Ah?

嘿嘿~~看來你找錯人了!

啊?

General Cayman !?

凱曼將軍!?

123

Cayman! How did you find this place!? This place is only known by the Royal Family!

凱曼！你怎樣找到這裏的？ 這地方只有皇族才知道！

Hehehe, someone led the way for me.

嘿嘿嘿，有人給我帶路啊。

Ahh!!

啊!!

Luna!?

Luna betrayed Kang and Samba and even her father!? Please stay tuned for the last chapter!

To be continued in SAMBA FAMILY 6

露娜!? 露娜竟然出賣剛仔、森巴，還有自己的父親!? 密切留意最終回！ 森巴FAMILY 6 待續

《大偵探福爾摩斯》
四字成語 101

看大偵探福爾摩斯，學習四字成語好輕鬆！

〔遍體鱗傷〕

〔化險為夷〕

每本收錄 101 個成語，
配合小遊戲和豐富例句，
提高閱讀及寫作能力！

《大偵探福爾摩斯》
英文填字遊戲

寓學習於遊戲！

以有趣的填字遊戲學習英文
生字。
分「熱身」、「過渡」及「挑
戰」三階段，由淺入深。
每個考驗附有「實用小錦
囊」，介
紹生字相
關文法知
識、中英對
照例句及西
方文化。

《大偵探福爾摩斯》
提升數學能力讀本
數學都可以這樣玩!

每本定價 $88

《提升數學能力讀本》參考小學數學的學習範疇製作,共有六卷,大家可按自己的數學程度,隨意由任何一卷讀起。

這六卷書沒有深奧的數學理論及沉悶的說明,但有冒險故事、名人漫畫及可於生活應用的數學,令大家輕鬆投入數學知識的領域中。

— ADVENTURE UNDER THE SEA!! — ⑤

Artist : Keung Chi Kit

Concept : Rightman Creative Team

Chief Editor : Chan Ping Kwan

Editors : Kwok Tin Bo, So Wai Yee, Wong Suk Yee

Designers : Wong Cheuk Wing, Yip Shing Chi

First published in Hong Kong in 2020 by

Rightman Publishing Limited

2A, Cheung Lee Industrial Building, 9 Cheung Lee Street, Chai Wan, Hong Kong

" SAMBA FAMILY ⑤ — ADVENTURE UNDER THE SEA!! — "
Copyright © 2020 Rightman Publishing Ltd./ Keung Chi Kit. All rights reserved.

Printed and bound by

Rainbow Printings Limited

3-4 Floor, 26-28 Tai Yau Street, San Po Kong, Kowloon, Hong Kong

Distributed by

Tung Tak Newspaper & Magazine Agency Co., Ltd.

Ground Floor, Yeung Yiu Chung No.5 Industrial Building, 34 Tai Yip Street,
Kwun Tong, Kowloon, Hong Kong
Tel: (852) 3551-3388   Fax: (852) 3551- 3300

This book shall not be lent, or otherwise circulated in any public libraries without publisher's
prior consent.

This publication is protected by international conventions and local law. Adaptation, reproduction or
transmission of text (in English or other languages) or illustrations, in whole or part, in any form or by any
means, electronic, mechanical, photocopying, recording or otherwise, or storage in any retrieval system
of any nature without prior written permission of the publishers and author(s) is prohibited.
This publication is sold subject to the condition that it shall not be hired, rented, or otherwise let out by
the purchaser, nor may it be resold except in its original form.

ISBN:978-988-8504-20-6

HK$60 / NT$270

If damages or missing pages of the book are found, please
contact us by calling (852) 2515-8787.

On-line purchasing is easy and convenient.
Free delivery in Hong Kong for one purchase above HK$100.
For details, please visit www.rightman.net.